Treasury
of
Classic
FAIRY TALES

with original illustrations by
MARIA MANTOVANI *and* RENZO BARSOTTI

Published in 2005 by Mercury Junior
20 Bloomsbury Street, London WC1B 3JH

© copyright 2001 text and illustrations McRae Books Srl
© copyright 2005 this edition Mercury Junior

Illustrations by Maria Mantovani, Renzo Barsotti

Designed and produced by Open Door Limited, Rutland

Title: Treasury of Classic Fairy Tales
ISBN: 1-84560-006-1

Treasury
of
Classic
FAIRY TALES

Mercury
Junior

Beauty
and the
Beast

nce upon a time there was a poor merchant who had three beautiful daughters. His two eldest daughters were proud and selfish, but his youngest daughter was clever and kind, and everyone called her Bella. One day the merchant and his family moved to a little house in the country.

Bella worked hard all day long, unpacking and cleaning the house, and making it comfortable to live in. Her sisters did not help her to do anything.

One day the merchant received a letter saying that one of his cargo ships had arrived in the port and was carrying many goods.

He was very happy and got ready to go to the city. His two eldest daughters begged him to bring them back some presents. Only Bella said she would miss him, and did not ask for anything. Just before he left, the merchant asked, "And you Bella, don't you want anything at all?"

"A rose!" she said finally, "it would make me very happy if you brought me back a rose, because roses don't grow here."

When the merchant arrived in the city, he discovered that he had to use the money he had made from his cargo ship to pay an old debt. He only had a little money left to buy his daughters some gifts.He found small gifts for his two eldest daughters, but he could not find a single flower for Bella.

Sadly, he left the city and he started his journey home. But his horse wandered off the path. It was freezing cold and it began to snow heavily. Then the poor, sad merchant saw a castle in the distance.

The front door was half open and the merchant went into the castle to ask

if he could warm his hands by the fire and perhaps have a little food. The

entrance hall was silent and deserted. He searched for a long time but did

not find anyone, so he decided to spend the night there and travel home in

the morning. He found a comfortable bed, pulled up the covers and fell asleep.

The next morning he woke up early, ready to go home, and went outside. As he crossed the gardens he saw a rosebush, which he had not noticed the night before. It was covered in beautiful roses. "What luck," he said to himself, "now I can take a present back for Bella too."

He had just picked the most beautiful rose when, suddenly, a horrible beast appeared and made a terrible roaring noise. He had claws and fur and piercing eyes. The merchant was terrified and could not say a word.

"I offer you the hospitality of my home and you repay me by stealing my flowers?" said the Beast. "I should kill you right now!" he growled. "Have pity on me!" cried the merchant, "this rose is for my daughter."

On hearing this, the Beast said, "Very well, I believe you. You are free to go, but instead of your life, you must send your daughter to live with me!" The merchant tried to dissuade him, but the Beast would not give in, so reluctantly, the merchant agreed.

He returned home full of dread. He did not know how he would explain

to Bella what had happened.

When he saw his daughters he gave them their presents, but he took Bella

to one side and told her, through his tears, his terrible story. Bella listened

carefully and bravely she said, "Don't worry Father. If this is what you

have promised to the Beast, I'll go and live in the castle."

The following morning the merchant took his daughter to the castle and, broken-hearted, he left her in the garden. Bella went into the castle and wandered nervously from room to room. Then she found a table covered with lots of delicious food.

Everything was so beautiful, and the food looked so good, that Bella almost forgot how much she missed her family. Then, all of a sudden, the Beast appeared.

She was horrified by his ugliness, but she greeted him politely. The Beast responded courteously and invited her to have lunch with him. They ate and talked until evening. Life at the castle was good and Bella grew to enjoy the company of the Beast. They spent many days talking, reading and walking in the garden together.

The Beast paid Bella a lot of attention and was very kind and gentle. She stopped noticing his ugliness.

When, however, the Beast asked for her hand in marriage, she replied, "I cannot accept, my dear friend. I am so fond of you but I cannot marry you." The Beast was very sad, but respected her decision.

Time passed, and Bella, although very happy at the castle, missed

her father and her sisters. Then the Beast gave her a magic mirror

as a present. He said she could see her family through it, so she would

not be so homesick.

18

One night Bella looked in the mirror and saw that her father was sick in bed. Tearfully, Bella begged the Beast to let her return home. "If that's what you wish, then go!" said the Beast, "but remember, when your father is well again, you must return to the castle or I'll die."

Bella promised to return as soon as she
could, thanked him, and rushed home
to look after her father. On seeing Bella
again, who he had missed greatly, the
merchant began to get better. Many
days passed and Bella was so happy to
be back with her family that she almost
forgot about the Beast.

One night Bella had a terrible dream.
She heard the voice of the Beast
begging her to return. Full of guilt,
Bella remembered her broken promise and decided to go back to the

castle. She was certain something terrible had happened and she wanted

to find the Beast.

Bella searched all over the castle for the Beast, but it was deserted.

Finally, she went into the garden and she found the Beast. He had

fallen to the ground and looked almost dead.

Bella suddenly realised how much she loved him and with tears running down her cheeks she hugged him. "Please don't die, I love you and I want to marry you," she wept.

Then, right before her eyes, the Beast was transformed into a handsome prince. He told her that an evil witch had turned him into a beast. "Only the love of a beautiful girl could break the spell," he explained, "you have saved me Bella. I want to marry you right away." And so, they married and lived happily ever after.

Cinderella

nce upon a time, there was a wealthy man and his young daughter. His wife had died some time ago and he decided to remarry to give his daughter a new mother. However, the woman he chose was cruel, and she had two equally cruel daughters.

The wicked stepmother and her daughters picked on the young girl, and made her do all the hardest household chores. She had to mop the floors, polish the silver and wash all their dirty clothes every day. She was so tired in the evenings that she did not notice that she was covered in cinders and ash. Her nasty half-sisters noticed though, and they called her Cinderella.

One day the king's son decided to throw a magnificent ball, and all the young women in the kingdom were invited.

As soon as they received their invitation, Cinderella's stepmother and half-sisters began to try on their most beautiful clothes and jewellery. Cinderella wanted to go too, but when she said so, her cruel half-sisters just laughed and said, "Certainly not! We don't want

to be embarrassed by a little wretch like you!"

Although Cinderella was very upset she did not let it show. On the

day of the ball she helped her half-sisters and stepmother to get ready.

She ironed their clothes, polished their shoes, fastened their petticoats,

and even helped them with their hair and make-up.

When evening finally came, a beautiful carriage drew up at the door to take them to the castle. Cinderella listened until the sound of the horses' hooves and carriage wheels had faded into the distance, then she ran to her room and burst into tears.

Suddenly a Kind Fairy appeared and said, "My dear child, why are you so sad? Tell me what is wrong and I'll see what I can do to help." Cinderella told her about the ball at the castle and how she wanted to go.

The Kind Fairy listened carefully, thought hard for a moment, and then said, "I know how we can get you to the ball! Now listen, I need a big pumpkin and some mice. Tell me where I can find them."

Cinderella took the Kind Fairy into the garden, where she chose the most beautiful pumpkin and gave it to her. Then she said, "Now bring me some mice!" Cinderella ran to get a mouse trap, where six little mice were trapped.

With a touch of her magic wand, the Fairy transformed the pumpkin into a golden coach and the mice into six beautiful white horses.

"Silly me!" said the Fairy, "I forgot the coachman and the pages!" And, quicker than you can say quick, she turned six lizards into six smartly-dressed pages and a big mole into a pot-bellied coachman. Cinderella could not believe her luck! The beautiful coach would take her to the castle where she would meet the Prince.

Then she said, "Dear Fairy, how can I go to the castle dressed like this?" The Kind Fairy smiled and touched her with her magic wand. In a flash, her rags turned into a beautiful dress fit for a princess, and her slippers into a dazzling pair of crystal shoes.

Cinderella was so happy in her beautiful clothes and she felt like a real princess!

As she waved goodbye, the Kind Fairy warned her to come home before

the clock struck midnight. She said that the spell would end at that time.

Cinderella thanked the Kind Fairy and promised that she would be back

in time.

Then she got into the carriage and set off towards the castle.

By the time Cinderella got to the castle all the other guests had arrived.

They were laughing and chatting and dancing, but as Cinderella entered

a hush fell over the ballroom. All the ladies and gentlemen turned to stare at the beautiful young woman.

"But who is she?" they whispered among themselves, "look at her gorgeous dress and her kind and elegant ways."

The Prince himself remarked that he had never seen such an enchanting young woman.

He immediately asked Cinderella to dance with him. They whirled around the room together, dancing and talking. The Prince was enthralled and danced with no one else the whole evening. The other women looked on with envy, but Cinderella was so happy she didn't notice.

The hours passed so happily that Cinderella forgot her promise to leave before midnight. Only when the great clock began to chime midnight did Cinderella remember that the spell was about to end.

Cinderella quickly bid farewell to the Prince and ran out of the ballroom,

much to everyone's surprise. As she dashed down the staircase one

of her beautiful crystal shoes fell off, but there was no time to stop and

pick it up. The astonished Prince tried to follow her, but all that was

left of the mysterious girl was a crystal shoe. He bent down to pick

it up and realised then and there that he had fallen in love with

the beautiful stranger.

By the time Cinderella reached the street it was past midnight and her

ball gown had turned to rags. Next to her lay the pumpkin and the six

white mice scuttled away into the dark.

Just as the Kind Fairy had told her,

the spell was over! Cinderella

made her way home through the

dark streets and fell asleep quickly.

The next morning, her stepmother and half-sisters told her all about the ball. They told her about the mysterious girl and how the king's son had fallen in love with her.

That day the Prince announced that he would marry the girl whose foot fit the crystal shoe worn by the lovely stranger.

A royal page travelled from house to house and every girl in the kingdom tried the shoe on. Cinderella's half-sisters tried the shoe too, but it did not fit. Only Cinderella's foot slipped easily into the crystal shoe.

The Prince was overjoyed! He and Cinderella were married a month later and they lived happily ever after in the beautiful castle.

Hansel

and

Gretel

nce upon a time a woodcutter and his wife lived with their two children near a big, dark wood. The little boy was called Hansel and the little girl Gretel. Their mother died when they were small and their father remarried.

Then there was a famine and the woodcutter did not know how to feed his family. "What will become of us? How can we feed our children, when we haven't enough for ourselves?" he asked his wife.

"Husband," she said, "we'll take the children into the woods and leave them there.

They'll never find their way home." "My poor children!" cried the woodcutter, "I can't leave them to die in the woods." But in the end his wife convinced him.

Hansel and Gretel,

who could not sleep for

hunger, overheard what their stepmother said. They were frightened.

Hansel crept outside and filled his pockets with shiny white pebbles.

The next morning the stepmother woke the children early and

they all set off for the woods. Gretel's apron held two small slices

of bread and Hansel's pocket

was bulging with

pebbles.

Every few steps Hansel turned and dropped a pebble on the path

behind him.

They came to the middle of the woods and the woodcutter made

a fire so they would not be cold. The stepmother said, "Now children,

lie down by the fire and rest until we come to take you home."

The children ate their bread and soon fell fast asleep.

When they woke up it was dark. Little Gretel began to cry. "How shall we find our way home?" she cried. But Hansel knew that they only had to wait for the moon to come up, and then the moonlight would show them the trail of pebbles that would lead them home. After a long time, they arrived home safe and sound, but it was well past midnight!

The children's father was overjoyed to have them back. But soon another famine came and the stepmother wanted to get rid of the children once and for all. "We'll take them even deeper into the woods," she said. Her husband was forced to agree.

Early next morning they set off again. This time Hansel crumbled the bread his stepmother had given him and dropped crumbs behind him, so that they would be able to find their way home.

46

Just as before, the children were left by a fire in the middle of the woods and they slept until dark.

But when the moon came up, they discovered that the birds had eaten the trail of breadcrumbs. They were lost! They wandered through the forest all night and all the next day, and the day after, and the day after that.

On the third morning they came to a clearing in the woods. There stood a lovely cottage made entirely of bread and cake and all kinds of sweets. Hansel and Gretel shouted for joy.

"Eat this!" said Hansel, handing his sister a slice of chocolate cake window sill, as he busily ripped a piece of candy off the roof for himself.

Just then a very old
woman came out of
the cottage.

"Ah, you dear little things," she said, "eat all you want and then come
inside to sleep. You can live with me now." At first the old woman was
kind to the children. But she was really a wicked witch and she planned
to cook them and eat them up as soon as they were fat enough.

She locked Hansel in a cage and made Gretel take him lots of food
to fatten him up. But Gretel was given almost nothing to eat.

One morning the wicked old witch decided it was time to boil Hansel up
for lunch. She told Gretel to bring water for the pot and to make a fire
under it. While the water was boiling, she told Gretel to climb into the
oven to see if it was hot enough to bake some bread. But what she really
wanted to do was slam the door behind her and cook her as well!

Little Gretel pretended she could not get into the oven. The old witch scolded her saying, "Stupid! Look how easy it is. Even I can do it!" As she clambered into the oven, Gretel gave her a huge shove and slammed the door shut.

"Hansel! Hansel!" she shouted, "we are saved! The wicked old witch is dead." She opened the cage and Hansel jumped out and hugged his sister. They both danced for joy.

Before they left the witch's house they filled their pockets and Gretel's apron with all the precious stones and gold she had collected over the years. Then they set off for home.

When they had walked for two hours they came to a big lake. There was no bridge and no boat, and the children did not know how to cross it. Then they saw a big white duck. They jumped onto its back and it took them quickly across the lake.

They walked for a little while longer and then they came to a well-known road. At long last they saw their father's house in the distance. They began to run.

They found their father alone in the house. His wife had died. He had been very sad since he left the children in the woods. The children hugged and kissed him. Then they showed him the treasure they had taken from the witch's house. And they all lived happily ever after!

Little Red
Riding Hood

Once upon a time there was a little girl who was very kind to everyone in her village. One day her grandmother, who loved her granddaughter very much, gave her a red riding cape with a big red hood.

The little girl thought her new cape was wonderful and she put it on straight away. She said she would wear it wherever she went. In such a bright colour, the little girl could be seen from far away, and very soon everyone began calling her Little Red Riding Hood.

Early one morning, Little Red Riding Hood's mother asked her to visit her grandmother, who was ill and needed medicine and food.

She gave her some fresh bread and a bottle of wine to take to her grandmother. "Go straight to your grandmother's house and don't go wandering in the wood," her mother warned.

"And when you get there, be polite and say 'Good Day' to your grandmother, and don't go looking into her drawers and wardrobe."

Little Red Riding Hood's grandmother lived

in a little cottage in the middle of a big wood quite

a long way from the village. It took about half an hour to get there.

So off Little Red Riding Hood went. She had just entered the wood

when she met a wolf. "Good Day Little Red Riding Hood," said the

Wolf. Since he was such a well mannered and handsome wolf, Little

Red Riding Hood replied politely, "Good Day Mr Wolf."

"Where are you going all by yourself so early

in the morning?" asked the Wolf. "To my grandmother's house.

She is ill and I am taking her this fresh bread and bottle of wine to help

her get better," she replied.

The Wolf was clever and he was really thinking that this little girl would make a tasty morsel. He did not frighten her, however, because he wanted to eat her grandmother too!

"Tell me, where does your grandmother live?" the Wolf asked.

"In a cottage about quarter of an hour's walk from here," said Little Red Riding Hood, who was always very polite.

"That's a good idea!" said Little Red Riding Hood.

Little Red Riding
Hood left the main
path and began
picking flowers.
She gathered a
large and beautiful
bunch for her
grandmother.

Then suddenly she

remembered her mother's words.

"Go straight to your grandmother's house," her mother had said.

Little Red Riding Hood went back to the path and started walking

to her grandmother's house.

In the meantime, the Wolf had left Little Red Riding Hood and

had found her grandmother's house. He knocked quietly on the door.

"Who's there?" asked the old lady.

"Little Red Riding Hood, Grandma. I have fresh bread and good wine from Mummy to make you feel better," the Wolf said in a high-pitched voice. "Open the door and let yourself in. I'm too sick to get out of bed."

The Wolf slowly opened the cottage door and leapt into the old lady's bedroom. Before the grandmother could call out for help, she had been swallowed up whole by the Wolf.

Little Red Riding Hood

Then the Wolf put on the grandmother's long nightgown and frilly nightcap, and clambered into her warm bed. He pulled the covers right up to his chin and waited.

A few minutes later Little Red Riding Hood arrived. She was a little surprised to find the door open. "Good Day Grandma," she called, but there was no reply. She went into the room to see if her grandmother was better or worse.

"But Grandma!" she exclaimed, "what big eyes you've got!" "All the better to see you with," came the reply.

"But Grandma! What a big nose you've got!" "All the better to smell you with," came the reply.

"But Grandma! What enormous teeth you've got!"

"All the better to eat you with!" growled the Wolf, who suddenly jumped out of bed and swallowed the poor girl whole.

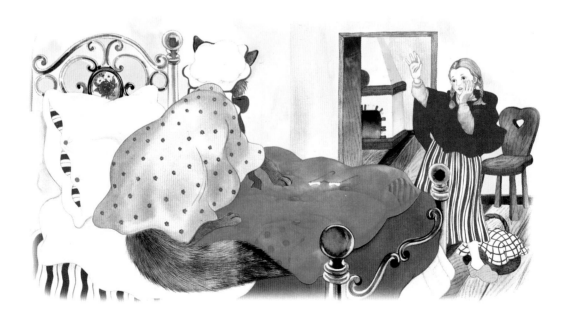

After so much food the Wolf felt very tired, so he climbed back into bed. He soon fell asleep and began to snore. The snoring was so loud that a huntsman, passing by the little cottage, heard the noise and decided to go and see if the old lady was well.

The huntsman went into the cottage and could not
believe his eyes. There was a Wolf wearing
a nightgown and frilly cap, fast asleep
in bed! Suddenly a strange sound
came from the Wolf's stomach.
The huntsman got out
his knife and cut
open the Wolf's
stomach.

And...surprise!
Out of the Wolf's
stomach came Little
Red Riding Hood
and her grandmother.
Although shaken by
their adventure, they were
both happy to be alive. The huntsman took them back to the village and
grandmother stayed with Little Red Riding Hood and her mother until

she was well again. They all lived happily together and forgot all about

the horrible Wolf.

Pinocchio

Once upon a time there was an old carpenter named Geppetto. He was very poor. One day he decided to make a puppet. He thought that if people liked the puppet he could sell many more.

He found a large piece of wood and set to work. First he carved the eyes, but he noticed a strange thing. The eyes were never still and kept watching him. Then he carved the nose. It started to grow and grow, forcing Geppetto to cut it again and again. Finally, he carved the mouth.

As soon as it was finished, the puppet began to laugh and make faces.

Geppetto named him Pinocchio.

When he was finished, Geppetto stood the puppet up. Pinocchio learned

to walk by himself in no time at all.

A few days later he was running through the streets like a little devil. Poor

Geppetto couldn't keep up! While he was chasing Pinocchio, he was arrested

by a policeman, who thought the old carpenter wanted to beat up the puppet.

Left by himself, Pinocchio went home. There he met a cricket who was very special.

He was none other than the very wise Talking Cricket. He warned Pinocchio against being a rascal and told him to be more respectful of his father Geppetto. Pinocchio, who didn't like being told what to do, threw a large hammer at the cricket to shut him up.

Geppetto wanted Pinocchio to go to school like all the other boys. So he made him some clothes out of wrapping paper and scraps of material. Pinocchio also needed a dictionary for school so that he could learn his ABCs. The good Geppetto, who was very poor, sold his own coat to buy Pinocchio a brand new one.

Pinocchio left for school full of good intentions.

But on the way, he was distracted by some very inviting music. It came from the Puppet Theatre, where a comedy was being staged. Pinocchio didn't have the money to go

in, so he sold the dictionary that Geppetto had just bought. When the

puppet actors saw him, they ran up to

him and greeted him warmly.

All of a sudden, Fire-eater, the terrible puppeteer, appeared. Angered by

the interruption, he snatched up Pinocchio to teach him a lesson.

Pinocchio, however, was able to move him to pity by telling him the story

of his poor father. Fire-eater, who was actually a kind-hearted man,

decided to let him go, and even gave him five gold coins for Geppetto.

On his way home, Pinocchio met the Cat and the Fox. They found out about the coins, and wanted to trick him out of them. They convinced Pinocchio that there was a place nearby called the "Field of Miracles". They said that whoever buried his money there would see trees full of gold coins spring up. Pinocchio was thrilled. He said goodbye to the Cat and the Fox, and headed for the miraculous site.

Shortly after, the two thieves, heavily
disguised, attacked Pinocchio and
tried to steal his coins. Luckily he had
hidden them in his mouth! When the
Cat and the Fox couldn't find the
coins they tied poor Pinocchio to a
tree and left him there.

The Blue Fairy, who lived nearby, rescued him. She took him home and took care of him.

Pinocchio tried to tell her about himself, but he told so many lies that his nose grew. The Blue Fairy scolded him and told him that boys should not tell lies. Then, to cheer him up, she called in some woodpeckers to peck his nose back to normal size.

When he felt better, Pinocchio set off for home. Unfortunately, he ran into the Cat and the Fox again. They had taken off their disguises and talked to him as if nothing had happened.

Pinocchio trusted them and went with them to the Field of Miracles. Following their advice, he buried the gold coins, certain that when he came back he would find trees laden with gold. But when he reached the field, he found neither the trees nor his coins. The Cat and the Fox had tricked him! After these misadventures, Pinocchio promised to never listen to bad advice, to always obey his father Geppetto and to become a good student.

Pinocchio kept his promises for a while. Then one day his classmate, Candlewick, asked him if he would like to go with him to the land of toys. The land of toys was a fantastic place. There were no schools and boys could play as much as they liked without being bothered by adults.

The two boys were happy for a few months until one day Pinocchio realised that his ears had grown into two long donkey's ears! Then he turned completely into a donkey. The same thing happened to his friend Candlewick.

The two little donkeys were taken to a market where Pinocchio was bought by a troupe of street performers to use in their shows. Then he was sold to a farmer, who wanted to use his skin to make a drum.

The farmer tied him with rope and threw him in the ocean to drown him.

Luckily, the Blue Fairy rescued Pinocchio and turned him into a puppet once again. The farmer, who didn't have any use for a piece of wood, untied him.

Pinocchio, who was nimble as ever, dove headfirst into the sea and swam away.

Unfortunately, at that very same moment an enormous whale was swimming by and swallowed him up. Imagine Pinocchio's surprise when, once inside the belly of the whale, he met none other than old Geppetto! The good man had been swallowed up some time before, while trying to cross the ocean in search of Pinocchio. Thrilled to have found his father, Pinocchio decided they must escape as soon as possible. That same night, taking advantage of the fact that the whale slept with her mouth open, they managed to make their getaway.

As time went by, Pinocchio became a more sensible boy. One night the Blue Fairy appeared to him in his dreams, and smilingly told him that she forgave him for all his past lies and mistakes. The next morning Pinocchio woke up, rubbed his eyes and to his great joy, realised that he had become a real boy made of flesh and blood. Right next to him, on the chair, was a funny wooden puppet.

Puss
in
Boots

nce upon a time there was a miller who had three sons. When the miller died, he left his sons the few things that he owned: a mill, a donkey and a cat named Puss in Boots. The youngest inherited Puss in Boots, the middle one got the mill and the eldest had the donkey. The youngest was unhappy with his inheritance, and complained about his rotten luck.

He feared he would die of hunger very soon, while his brothers would prosper thanks to their mill and donkey. Hearing him complain, Puss in Boots, who was a fairly special cat, told him: "Don't worry! Bring me a sack and a nice pair of boots, and everything will work out just fine."

The boy was a bit puzzled, but decided to trust Puss in Boots and hurried

to get what he needed. Wearing his nice boots and carrying the sack on

his shoulder, Puss in Boots went into the woods where many wild animals

lived. He scattered some fresh grass in the sack and placed it on the

ground. Then he hid in the bushes to wait for a hungry hare to hop inside

the sack for a snack.

Soon a young hare, attracted by the scent of the grass, walked into the

trap. Puss in Boots jumped out of his hiding place, grabbed the sack,

closed it carefully and set out towards the king's castle.

When he arrived at court,

Puss in Boots asked to be received

by the king. After many bows, he produced the hare and said:

"Your Majesty, please accept this as a personal gift from the Marquis

of Carabas" (this was the name he had made up for his master).

The king gladly accepted the hare and asked Puss in Boots to thank the

Marquis of Carabas. A few days later Puss in Boots went hunting in a

cornfield. Using the sack, he captured two partridges, and, just as before,

gave them to the king. For two or three months Puss in Boots kept taking

all sorts of wild game to the castle, and each and every time he told the

king that they were gifts from his master.

One day Puss in Boots learned that the king was going for a ride in the
royal carriage with his daughter. He rushed to his master and said:

"Master, you must go swimming in the river. I'll show you where.

Don't worry. Trust me!"

The boy, who by then had decided to follow Puss in Boots' advice,

however odd, went to the river. He dove in and waited. After a little

while the king and the beautiful princess came by in their carriage.

Puss in Boots immediately started shouting at the top of his voice:

"Help, help! The Marquis of Carabas is drowning!"

Hearing his cries, the king ordered the carriage to stop and asked his guards to help the poor Marquis. In the meantime, Puss in Boots had hidden his master's ragged clothes. He ran up to the king and said: "Thank you, Your Majesty, for having saved my master, but the poor man has no clothes. Thieves stole them while he was bathing!"

The king ordered that some of his own beautiful garments be sent from the castle and offered them as a gift to the Marquis of Carabas.

The Marquis of Carabas looked very handsome dressed in the king's elegant clothing. When the king's daughter saw him, she fell in love. The king, delighted by the boy's good manners, invited him into the carriage to ride with them.

Puss in Boots, very pleased about the way things were going, ran ahead of the carriage at full speed.

As he ran, he saw some farmers cutting grass in a field. He stopped and told them: "The king is about to ride by. When he asks you who owns the land, tell him the owner is the Marquis of Carabas. If you don't, you'll be sliced up into tiny pieces!"

When the king rode by, he asked the farmers who owned the well-tended fields. Frightened by Puss in Boots' threats, the farmers answered that they belonged to the Marquis of Carabas. The king was favourably impressed, and told the Marquis so.

Puss in Boots ran on ahead and this time stopped in front of some
farmers harvesting corn in a field. He told them: "The king is about
to ride by. When he asks you who owns all this corn, tell him it belongs
to the Marquis of Carabas. If you don't, you'll be punished and
sliced up into tiny pieces!"

After a little while the king rode by and asked the farmers who owned the corn. Scared by Puss in Boots' threats, the farmers answered that the owner was the Marquis of Carabas. Again the king congratulated the Marquis. Puss in Boots kept running ahead and repeating the same threat to everyone he met. The king was more and more impressed by the Marquis of Carabas' vast possessions.

In the meantime, Puss in Boots reached a big castle where a very rich ogre lived. The ogre also happened to be the true owner of all the fields the king had seen.

Puss in Boots, who had heard about the ogre's special powers, asked to be received by him. He said to the ogre: "I've heard that you can transform yourself into any sort of animal. I don't really believe it and I'd like to see what you can do. Why don't you turn into an elephant or a lion, for instance?" The ogre, irked by the cat's words, turned into a terrifying lion.

Puss in Boots jumped up on a ledge and only came down when the ogre had turned back into himself. Then he taunted him again. "You might be able to turn yourself into a lion, but I don't think you could turn into something as small as a mouse, for instance!"

The ogre was now very angry, and turned himself immediately into a tiny mouse. Puss in Boots pounced on him at once and ate him up.

Meanwhile, the king had

reached the castle gates and,

pleased by its appearance, decided to stop in and visit. As soon as

Puss in Boots heard the sound of the royal carriage, he rushed out

to greet the king. "Welcome, Your Majesty!", he said with a bow.

"Welcome to the castle of the Marquis of Carabas." The king,

impressed by the castle's size, asked to see every room, and showered

the Marquis with praise.

The king was pleased by the Marquis' great riches and asked

him to marry his daughter.

The wedding ceremony was celebrated right away and the young

couple lived happily ever after.

Sleeping
Beauty

nce upon a time, in a kingdom far, far away, there lived a king and queen who wanted more than anything to have a child. After many years, their wish was granted and the queen gave birth to a beautiful baby girl.

The king was so happy that he decided to celebrate the event with a great party. He ordered a banquet and called the best musicians in the kingdom to court. The castle, lit-up for the occasion, welcomed the best families in the land.

For her christening, the little princess was visited by her godmothers, the seven good fairies of the kingdom. When the ceremony was over, all the guests were invited to a magnificent ballroom, where they ate and danced merrily far into the night.

Before leaving, each fairy gave the child a gift. The first gave her beauty, the second intelligence, the third generosity and so on, until each one had given her all the best blessings in the world.

When it was the last fairy's turn, an old witch, whom no one had invited, entered the ballroom. Offended because she had not been invited, she went to the crib and said:

"I want to give the little princess something too. The child will live until the age of sixteen, when she will prick her finger on a spindle and die!" After casting her terrible curse the witch disappeared. The king and queen were devastated.

Then the seventh good fairy said: "My power isn't strong enough to reverse the witch's curse, but I can lessen it."

"My gift to your daughter will be that she pricks herself with the spindle, but she won't die. She will fall into a deep sleep that will last for one hundred years. Then a prince will wake her up with a kiss." That same day the king ordered all the spindles in the kingdom to be burned, and from then on, owning a spindle was strictly forbidden.

Time passed and the princess grew up to be beautiful, intelligent and loved by all. The curse of the evil witch was almost forgotten. One day the princess, who had just turned sixteen, decided to explore the castle. One by one she looked in each room until she reached an isolated turret where no one ever went. At the top of the turret was a little door. Curious, the princess opened it and entered a tiny room where an old lady was spinning wool with a spindle.

The woman had lived alone for many years. She had never heard of the princess and did not know that spindles were forbidden. The princess, fascinated by the strange object, went to her and asked: "What are you doing, dear lady?" "I'm spinning wool, my dear," answered the old lady. "That looks like fun!"

"Would you be so kind as to let me try?" said the girl. Alas, as soon as she touched the spindle she pricked her finger and fell to the ground. The old lady was terrified and ran down the stairs to look for help.

The king and queen ran to the little room with doctors and servants, but all their efforts to wake the princess were in vain. The curse had taken effect, and the princess would only wake up after one hundred years. The king summoned the seventh fairy, while his daughter was brought to the most beautiful room in the palace.

When the fairy arrived, she found the princess sleeping peacefully just as she had predicted.

Then she realised that the princess would wake up in one hundred years

time and would no longer find any of the people she loved.

The beautiful princess would be sad and all alone in the huge castle.

And so it was that the fairy decided that all the people of the palace

should sleep until the princess' re-awakening.

She went room by room, touching everyone with her magic wand.

Waiters, governesses, cooks, gardeners, soldiers and horses all gently

slipped away into a deep slumber.

When all was shrouded in silence the fairy left the castle, and with

another spell had a thick thorny hedge grow up around it. In time

it became so tall and dense that it enveloped the entire castle, making

it impossible for anyone to go inside.

One hundred years later a prince who was hunting in the area came upon the castle overgrown with thorns. Curious, he asked an old man if he knew who the owner was.

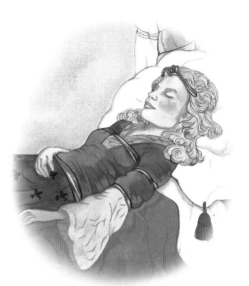

The old man answered that a beautiful princess had been sleeping in the castle for many years, and that only a prince could wake her up. Fearing the curse, no one had ever dared go near it.

Proudly, with his sword drawn, the prince made his way through the thick, prickly underbrush.

To his surprise, the trees and thorn bushes opened before him, leaving
a long avenue that led to the castle.

As the young prince went forward, the trees closed behind him, making
it impossible for anyone to follow. When he reached the palace, he was
struck by the strange stillness. As he looked for the princess he realised
the reason for the eerie silence: all the castle's occupants were sound
asleep!

The prince searched every room, and finally came upon the princess, lying in her bed surrounded by soft pillows.

She looked so beautiful that he went up to her and gently kissed her face. The princess opened her eyes and smiled.

The young couple fell in love and decided that they would get married that very same day. Suddenly everyone in the castle woke up from their long sleep.

A great party was held to celebrate the wedding and the prince and princess lived happily ever after.

114

Snow White

and the

Seven Dwarfs

Once upon a time in the heart of winter a queen sat sewing at her castle window. Distracted by the heavy snowfall, she pricked her finger with the needle. Several drops of bright red blood stained the snow on the window sill. The red looked so beautiful against the pure white snow and the queen thought: "Oh how I would love to have a child with skin as white as snow, lips as red as blood and hair as black as ebony!"

After a while, the queen gave birth to a daughter who was everything she had wished for. The queen herself died soon afterwards. The child was called Snow White.

A year later, Snow White's father, the king, married a beautiful but cruel and proud woman. The new queen could not bear anyone to be more beautiful than she was.

The queen had a magic mirror and she would stand in front of it and ask the same question: "Mirror Mirror on the wall, who is the fairest of them all?" And the mirror would reply: "You, Mistress, are the fairest of them all." And the Queen was happy.

The years passed and Snow White grew up. She was an intelligent and lovely child. At seven years old she was more beautiful than her stepmother. One day, as usual, the queen asked the mirror: "Mirror, Mirror on the wall, who is the fairest of them all? The mirror replied: "Mistress, to tell the truth is my only duty. Now Snow White has the most beauty." The queen was furious, and hated Snow White with all her heart.

The queen hated Snow White so much that one day she ordered
a huntsman to take her into the forest and murder her. But when they
reached the middle of the woods Snow White began to cry and the
huntsman took pity on her. She promised never to return to the castle
and he set her free.

Snow White was all alone and afraid. She ran through the forest until she
could run no more. It was getting dark when she saw a little cottage and
decided to go inside and rest.

Inside the cottage everything was in order, although strangely small. The table was laid with seven little plates and seven little glasses, and in another small room there were seven little beds all in a row. Snow White was very hungry. She ate from one of the little plates and drank from one of the tiny cups.

After eating and drinking, Snow White felt very tired, so she lay down on one of the tiny beds and was soon fast asleep.

The cottage was owned by seven dwarfs who worked all day in the
mountains, looking for precious stones. When they came home that night
they saw that someone had eaten from one of their plates and drunk from
one of their cups.

To their astonishment, they found a little girl asleep in one

of their beds and, stunned by her beauty, they decided to let her

sleep until the morning.

When Snow White woke up, the dwarfs were very kind to her, and asked

how she had come to be in their little cottage. She told them her story and

the dwarfs, who were good men, invited her to stay with them. In return

for their hospitality, Snow White looked after their little cottage.

In the meantime, the queen, who was convinced that Snow White was

dead, asked the mirror the same question: "Mirror, Mirror on the wall,

123

who is the fairest of them all?" and the mirror replied: "Mistress, here you have beauty it is true, but in the woods Snow White has more beauty than you."

When the queen realised that Snow White was still alive she was filled with rage and she decided to kill the girl herself.

Using magic, the queen prepared a poisonous apple and transformed herself into an old woman. She went to the cottage of the seven dwarfs and knocked. Snow White opened the door and when she saw the beautiful red apple that the old lady was offering she gladly took it.

Snow White started eating the apple but with the very first bite she dropped down dead. The queen, happy that her beautiful rival was no more, returned to the castle and asked the mirror:

"Mirror, Mirror on the wall,
who is the fairest of them
all?" And finally she was
given the reply she desired:
– "The queen! She is the
most beautiful of all."

That evening, when the seven dwarfs came home after
work, they found Snow White dead on the floor.
In despair, they tried everything they could think
of to bring her back to life, but to no avail.

127

Full of sorrow, they decided not to bury her, but to lay her in a crystal coffin so that everyone could admire her beauty. They placed the coffin on a hillside and all the animals wept when they saw that Snow White was dead.

One day, a prince passed by and saw the coffin resting on the hillside and the beautiful girl who lay inside. He fell in love with Snow White and decided to take her with him.

The seven dwarfs did not want to be separated from her, but the young man insisted until, at last, they agreed. Then the prince made arrangements for Snow White to be carried back to his castle.

As they carried her, the path became rocky and the journey was bumpy.

Suddenly, a piece of apple was knocked out of Snow White's mouth.

She had never swallowed that first bite of the poisoned apple.

To everyone's joy, Snow White opened her eyes and and began to wake up.

Confused and sleepy, she did not know what had happened. The prince explained everything to her and told her he loved her and that he wanted to marry her. Snow White was very happy and agreed to the marriage.

The happy couple were married a short time later. A great wedding feast was held at the prince's castle and everyone had a wonderful time. And the wicked Queen? What became of her? She died of envy!

The
Three
Little Pigs

Once upon a time there were three little pigs who were cheerful and carefree. They all lived with their mother in a little house at the edge of a forest. In time, the three little pigs grew bigger and the little house became too small. One day they decided to build better houses that were big enough and more pleasant.

Their mother gave them her blessing and told them not to forget the dangers of the forest: "Be careful, my children, of the hungry wolf who lives in the woods!" "Do not worry Mummy", said the three brothers all together, but they were a little afraid as they began their journey to find a new place to live.

133

After a while, the wolf, who had watched this scene, rubbed his hands together, convinced that before evening he would have gobbled the three little pigs up. The three brothers went deeper into the forest.

The smallest pig, as well as the most cheerful, ran after a butterfly, stopped to look at the squirrels and to imitate with his flute the sounds of the birds. The biggest pig loved to sing and whistle and walked along, looking at every leaf and every tree, playing on his violin, the tune his brother played on the flute.

"Our houses must be solid and well built to protect us from the wolf" said the biggest pig. "Yes yes, that's what Mummy said", agreed the other two.

The smallest pig, who liked being lazy, decided that his house should have walls of straw. The second brother, who was lazy too, would build his of wood.

The third pig, shook his head, saying that his house would be built of solid bricks. And all the while something fierce, with two big eyes, watched them from a distance.

In no time at all, the house of the littlest pig was finished. He was very pleased with himself and went proudly to help the second brother who had almost finished hammering a nail into the last piece of wood. Both of them had built their houses in a hurry, and were happy. They went to play music for their big brother, who, in spite of the effort, sang cheerfully, putting one brick on top of another.

"Do you think you will have finished before it gets dark?" called the two brothers, ridiculing him, while they skipped and ran and played. He just waved at his brothers and carried on building his house properly.

Returning to his house of straw, the littlest pig carried on playing his

flute. He played three notes, and the birds in the forest responded with

three notes of their own. The pig and the birds continued making music

until, at last, the final note was played and the forest became silent.

"What a beautiful house!" said a loud and terrible voice. "Who is there?"

cried the little pig. "A friend" called the voice, more softly. "I'm hungry,

let me in lovely pig." "B...But you are the wolf! Go away and do not try

to get in!" But the wolf took a deep breath and he huffed and he puffed

and he blew the house down. There was nothing left of the straw house that had been built too quickly. The little pig escaped just in time and ran

into the second brother's house built of wood.

"Come no further," said the second brother to the wolf. "In this house we

are safe and secure," and he quickly shut the door. How terrifying! But a

house made of wood must be better than a house of straw, thought the

pigs. The wolf was calm and happy to wait, thinking that they would soon

come out to play again.

"Come out little pigs, come and play with me."But the little pigs remembered what had happened to the house of straw and would not go out to play. "All right then, I will have to blow down this house of wood as well!" said the wolf. And he huffed and he puffed, and he huffed and he puffed until, at last, he blew the house down.

The two little pigs ran and ran and ran until they got to their big brother's house made of bricks.

"Come in, don't be afraid," said their big brother. You will be safe here with me." "Are you sure?" whimpered the other two. "The wolf is strong and has powerful breath." But the biggest pig said "Huffing and puffing will not blow my house of bricks down, don't worry."

Perhaps they were saved, perhaps the wolf would eat all three of them, thought the three little pigs. Then the flute and the violin were no longer played, all that could be heard was the chattering of the frightened little pigs' teeth.

The wolf was outside and he was starving. "I will blown down this house as well!" he cried. "Before evening I will have all three of you lovely little pigs in my stomach." He took a deep breath and he huffed and he puffed but the house did not blow down.

So he took an even bigger breath and he huffed and he puffed, but nothing happened. Then he took an enormous breath, and he huffed and he puffed as hard as he could, but the house stood firm.

What a relief for the three little pigs! "There is nothing you can do! Nothing at all!" they sang in chorus. Then the wolf climbed onto the roof of the house and started to climb down the chimney. "Now I am coming to eat you!"

The three little pigs were frightened and miserable. But the biggest pig did not give up. "Come and put some wood in the fireplace." The other two looked bewildered, but did as they were told without asking a single question .

"Good, now light the fire." said their big brother. "When the wolf climbs down the chimney he will be sorry, you will see!" After having done this, the three little pigs fanned the flames higher and higher with bellows.

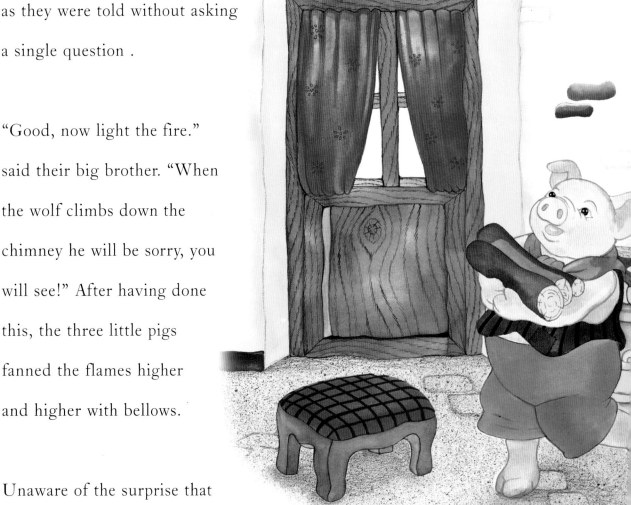

Unaware of the surprise that awaited him, the wolf lowered himself further down the chimney, becoming blacker and blacker from the soot and the smoke. The three little pigs saw the tip of a tail appear in the fireplace. Were they safe? How frightening! But then they heard a

terrible cry. The flames had reached the fur on the wolf's hind legs.

"Help! I am burning!" shrieked the wolf in the fireplace, rushing back up the chimney as fast as he could, and looking like a cannon ball being shot out of a cannon.

The wolf ran. He ran far, far away as fast as he could, with his tail smoking behind him. The three little pigs stood in the doorway of the house and watched him disappear in the distance.

Safe at last, the three little pigs stepped outside of the safe little house built of bricks, hugged each other and laughed. They sang and danced. They played music for the birds and were happy because the wolf that had nearly eaten them had gone.

Tired from laughing and dancing, at last, the three little pigs thought about their frightening adventure. "And now?"said the littlest pig. "We need another house." "Exactly." cried the second little pig. "Better than my house of wood."

"Dear brothers,"

said the oldest pig,

"I think that this time we

should all work together to build a beautiful and safe house. With solid walls and a wonderful fireplace. You must give me a hand." And so they did, and they were never troubled by the wolf again.

Thumbelina

Many many years ago, in a far away country, lived a woman whose greatest wish was to have a child. Unfortunately, she could not have one. So she spoke with a witch, who told her: "You mustn't worry! Do you see this magic seed? You must plant it in a pot and water it carefully. Wait and see!"

The woman ran home and did what the witch had told her. The following morning, when she got up, she saw that a great red and yellow tulip had sprung up from the seed.

The flower was still closed, but it was so beautiful that the woman kissed it. With a smacking sound, the petals opened, and a tiny little girl appeared inside the flower.

The woman took her delicately in her hands and said: "I'm going to call you Thumbelina because you're so tiny that you're no taller than my thumb!" Time went by and the little girl lived happily, surrounded by the woman's loving care. At night Thumbelina slept in a nutshell and used a rose petal as a pillow and a violet as a blanket. During the day she enjoyed playing in a plate full of water, pretending that the tulip petal was her boat.

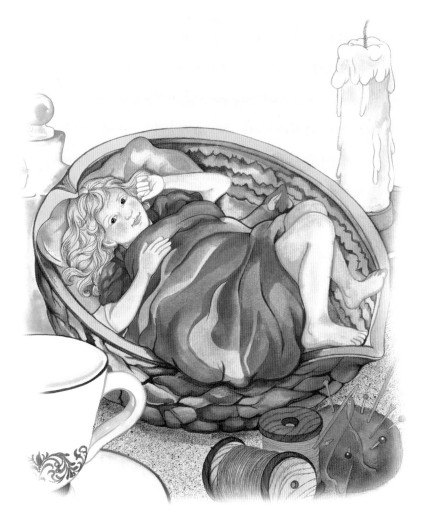

One night while the little girl was resting in her crib, an ugly toad hopped

on the window sill, and watched Thumbelina sleeping among the petals

from the open window. "She really is lovely!" thought the toad. "I think

she'd be an excellent wife for my son!" Without hesitation she hopped on

the table, grabbed the nutshell with Thumbelina and hopped back down

into the garden.

When she arrived at the swamp where she lived with her son, she set
Thumbelina on top of a water lily leaf in the middle of the pond.

"She won't be able

to escape from here," thought

 the big toad. "I'll keep her here until the wedding day." When she
woke up Thumbelina started crying, and when the toad announced
her wedding-to-be, she grew desperate.

Luckily the fish had heard everything. They decided to help Thumbelina:

bite after bite, they chewed up the stem of the leaf she was kept prisoner

on. When the leaf was finally

free it floated away, carried

by the current.

Thumbelina had just breathed a sigh of relief for her escape, when a

big may-beetle, attracted by her tiny size, grabbed her and took her away

with him on a tree branch. The insects who lived on the tree immediately

surrounded her and began laughing and teasing her: "What a strange

creature! Look, she only has two legs" said one. "How funny she is,

she doesn't even have antennas!" said the other. "She really is ugly!"

they shouted all together.

The may-beetle, irritated by the criticisms, took Thumbelina and dumped her without further ado in the middle of a huge field.

Thumbelina found herself once again in an unknown place, but this time she did not meet any unfriendly creatures. She slept among the flowers, feeding on their nectar and drinking their dew in the morning. Birds, song and sunshine filled her days. But the summer was soon over and the autumn as well.

The flowers wilted and the trees lost their leaves. All the animals holed-up in their dens or left for warmer places. Thumbelina was left all alone and with the arrival of snow, she was in danger of freezing. So she began looking for shelter, until one day she found a little door in a cornfield, and knocked on it hoping for some hospitality.

It was old Mrs. Mouse's den. Taking pity on the girl's state, she asked her to stay with her until the end of the winter. Thumbelina in return would take care of the house chores and keep Mrs. Mouse company by telling her stories. Time went by happily but for Thumbelina, used to the sun and song of the birds, staying cooped up in that den, where nothing ever happened, was very boring. One day Mrs. Mouse invited one of her neighbours, Mr. Mole.

She dusted off her most elegant tea service, prepared some pastries and told Thumbelina: "A dear friend is coming over today. Please treat him politely. He is an extremely distinguished gentleman who lives nearby in a very spacious underground den. His house has all the comforts and he is a millionaire. But he lives alone and has no company."

Actually Mrs. Mouse thought that Mr. Mole would be an excellent husband for Thumbelina and wanted them to meet to see if she could arrange a marriage. Thumbelina was very polite, answered every question and told the best stories she knew; Mr. Mole was enchanted by so much grace and decided to marry her.

A few days later, to return the visit, Mr. Mole went to pick up

Mrs. Mouse and Thumbelina and escort them to his den.

In the dark gallery connecting the two dens lay a dead bird,

who had presumably sought refuge there from the cold weather.

The three of them had to step over it and Thumbelina noticed that it was

a beautiful swallow, who hadn't migrated in time and had been killed by

the winter's chill.

Thumbelina was very sad about the dead bird, so that same night, when

Mrs. Mouse had fallen asleep, she slipped quietly out of bed to say a final goodbye to the swallow. It was then that she realised that the swallow's heart was still beating. Thumbelina leapt with joy and rushed to look for something to eat and for some covers to warm her up.

All winter long Thumbelina secretly tended the swallow, who gradually began to get her strength back. In the spring the bird was ready to fly again. When it was time to say goodbye, Thumbelina became very sad and the swallow offered to take her away with her. "I would gladly come, but I can't leave Mrs. Mouse alone! She has been so kind to me!" answered the girl tearfully.

After the swallow's departure Thumbelina's life went on as before; every once in a while she was allowed to take a peek outside from the den's entrance, and she would search the sky hoping to see her friend the swallow. But the times she was allowed to look outside were few and far between, because Mrs. Mouse did not want Thumbelina to leave the den. Finally, at the end of the summer, Mrs. Mouse called her and said: "Mr. Mole asked for your hand and wants to marry you at the start of the winter."

Thumbelina, trembling with displeasure, said that she would never agree to the wedding. But the old lady would not listen and immediately started tailoring her trousseau and wedding dress.

Thumbelina was miserable. She thought that her friend the swallow could have helped her, but she didn't know how to find her.

Just when she had given up all hope, she heard someone calling her. It was the swallow, who had come by to see her and thank her once more before setting out for warmer climates.

161

Thumbelina told her that soon enough she would have to marry Mr. Mole and she would be forced to live in an ugly underground den, where there was no sun. "Come with me," said the swallow. "I'll take you to a wonderful country where the sun always shines and the flowers never wilt!"

Thumbelina hopped on the swallow and they flew away together. They flew over oceans, plains and tall mountains, and finally arrived in a valley with an immense field of flowers. The swallow landed and deposited the girl on a white flower in full bloom.

162

As soon as

Thumbelina touched its

petals the flower opened and a

handsome young man appeared, no taller

than a thumb.

He wore a gold crown on his head, and from behind his shoulders two

small transparent wings stood out: he was the king of this fantastic country.

The little king fell in love with Thumbelina and asked her to marry him.

Thumbelina said yes. Suddenly swarms of small winged creatures flew out

from the flowers in the field to pay tribute to the new queen, bringing her

as a gift two splendid wings with which to fly all over her new kingdom.

Town Mouse

and

Country

Mouse

On a beautiful summer's day a rather distinguished town mouse decided to visit a distant relative who lived in the country. The two cousins spent a day or two together, then the town mouse set off again for the city.

On his way back, the town mouse stopped to rest in the shade. He rested his head against a tree trunk and fell asleep. All of a sudden he was woken by a noise.

Looking around, he saw that he was being observed by a country mouse. The country mouse came up to him and said very politely: "Good evening! I'm sorry to bother you, but it's getting dark and I thought perhaps you might need shelter for the night. I live nearby and would be very happy to have you as my guest."

The town mouse eyed the stranger suspiciously, but he accepted the invitation anyway because he did not like travelling at night and the city was still far away.

The country mouse lived in a den at the foot of an oak tree. His house was very humble, but everything was clean and well kept. The city mouse looked around disdainfully.

In the meantime the country mouse was busy making dinner for his guest.

When it was ready, he invited him to the table and said: "Help yourself!"

But the city mouse didn't really like the country mouse's specialties, and he only nibbled a few things out of politeness.

When dinner was over, the two mice talked. The town mouse went on and on about the advantages of town life, such as nice houses and refined food.

The country mouse listened carefully and then said: "Why don't you stay for a few days? You'll find that life is very nice and pleasant here as well."

The town mouse accepted because he was curious to find out what life in the country was really like.

The town mouse opened his suitcase and settled himself into his room. "Tomorrow we'll get up early and go in the woods and fields to search for food," the country mouse told him.

172

Early next morning they were out in the woods. The country mouse introduced the town mouse to all his friends. Among them were a mole and a leveret, both very nice and excellent neighbours.

The country mouse was very pleased with his life and he never felt bored. He liked simple things and enjoyed living outdoors. But the town mouse hated getting up early to look for food.

The long walks tired him out and he did not enjoy meeting all the woodland creatures. So one morning he told the country mouse: "Dear friend, thank you for your hospitality, but I think it's time for me to go home."

He added: "To return your kindness, I'd like for you to come and stay with me for a while." The country mouse accepted and together they got on the first city-bound carriage.

When they arrived, the country mouse was immediately struck by the noise on the city streets and he felt suffocated by the tall buildings all around.

Dodging the carriage wheels and the many passers-by, the town mouse led his friend to his elegant den in an apartment downtown. As they scuttled through the doors, the country mouse thought he would finally be safe.

But as soon as they got inside, they were attacked by an enormous broom that tried to sweep them away. They just managed to reach the den before it got them.

The country mouse was so terrified that he didn't want to leave the den at all. But the town mouse convinced him to come out and they went to a very well-stocked pantry where they could, without too much effort, feast on all sorts of delicious food.

They ate to their hearts' content, but though he was very impressed by the lavish amounts of food, the country mouse wasn't at all at ease and missed the quiet of his home.

As they were

returning to the

town mouse's den a huge

cat suddenly appeared.

"This is the last straw," exclaimed

the country mouse. "I'm going home! You may

live in luxury," he said to the town mouse, "but my

life is much happier and more peaceful."

179

The Ugly Duckling

ow beautiful the countryside was in summer! The wheat was yellow, the oats were green and the hay was stacked up in the meadows.

The sunshine fell warmly on an old farmhouse surrounded by deep canals and thick woods. Down by the water's edge, hidden from view, Mother Duck brooded on her nest full of eggs.

Mother Duck felt tired and lonely. It seemed her eggs would never hatch.
Then, at last, they began to crack and one little duckling after another
popped out. Just one large egg remained.

Mother Duck's neighbours said it was a turkey's egg and told her
to leave it. "I've been sitting so long, that another day or two won't
matter," she thought. The great egg burst at last. "Peep, peep!" said
the little one as it tumbled out. But, oh, how large and ugly it was!

The next day Mother Duck decided to take her brood to the farmyard.

She led them down to the canal. Splash! She went into the water.

"Quack, quack!" she said, and one after the other the ducklings joined her.

Even the Ugly Duckling could swim. So he was not a turkey!

The ducks in the yard commented in loud voices:

"What a fine family. Only that big grey

one is very ugly!" The poor duckling

was teased and bitten, pecked and

chased by all the other ducks

and the hens as well.

Even his brothers and

sisters behaved unkindly.

They were always saying,

"Hope the cat gets you,

you ugly thing!"

His mother said she wished he had never been born.

The girl who fed the poultry kicked at him.

One day the Ugly Duckling ran away. Through hedges and across fields, he ran on and on until he came to a wide moor. He lay down among the reeds and slept, while the wild ducks looked on and shook their heads over his ugliness.

Bang! bang! A gun went off near where he slept. There was a great shooting party and the moor was teeming with hunters and dogs.

A fierce dog came up to the duckling. He thrust his nose at him, and bared his big white teeth. Then, splash, splash, and he was gone. "I am so ugly that not even a dog will bite me," thought the Ugly Duckling.

When the hunt was over the Ugly Duckling fled the moor as fast as he could. Towards evening he reached a wretched old hut. It was so shabby that it didn't know which side to fall over on and so remained standing.

In the hut lived an old woman, her cat and a hen. The old woman thought the duckling might lay eggs so she let him stay. "Can you purr?" asked the cat. "Can you lay eggs?" asked the hen. "How ugly you are," they both said.

The duckling couldn't lay eggs or purr,

so he left the old woman's house.

Autumn came. The leaves turned yellow and brown. The wind caught

them up and danced them about. The air was cold and the clouds were

heavy with hail and snow. The little duckling was afraid.

One evening, just as the sun was setting, a flock of large birds rose from among the reeds. The duckling had never seen anything so beautiful before. Their plumage was a dazzling white, and they had long slender necks. They were swans. They uttered strange cries, spread their broad wings, and flew away from the cold winter to warmer lands far over the seas.

The duckling felt very strange watching them. He turned round and round in the water and sent forth such a strange cry that he startled himself. He could not forget the beautiful birds.

Winter came and the duckling had to keep moving in the water to stop it from freezing. Every night the opening grew smaller and smaller. Finally, he was too tired to move and lay stiff and frozen in the ice.

Next morning a farmer found him and took him home. The duckling soon revived. The farmer's children wanted to play with him but he was frightened. In his terror he upset a milk pail and left feathers in the butter. The farmer's wife chased him away with a broom.

191

The winter was very long and hard. It would be too sad to tell of all the trouble and misery the duckling suffered. When spring came he tried his wings. They were much stronger now and before he knew it he was flying. After a short flight he landed in a lovely garden full of the fragrance of apple-blossom.

Three swans were gliding about on the pond. They were so lovely that the duckling flew towards them. "I am so ugly they will surely kill me," he thought.

He landed on the water, and swam towards the beautiful creatures.

They saw him and shot forward to meet him.

As he bowed his head
in shame, he caught
a glimpse of himself
in the water. He was
no longer a plump,
ugly, grey duckling.
He was a beautiful
swan! The other
swans swam round
him, stroking him
with their beaks.
He was very happy.

Just then some children ran into the garden carrying bread.

"Oh look! There is a new one!" And they clapped

their hands and shouted for joy. "The new one

is the best," they cried. "He is so young and

handsome!" The young swan was very happy. But

he was not proud, for a good heart is never proud.

195